Copyright

Summertime in Florida is a special place, the sun is out, and everything is green and vibrant. This is where Rhys and Ciaran start their story. They've just moved from the cold winters in Washington DC, to sunny Florida where they have a new house and a big yard to explore. They've brought their pets Jazzy, the basset hound, and Jellybean, the cockatiel, with them to start this new adventure with them.

"Why don't you boys go out and play in the backyard, it's a nice day out?" Mom said.

The both looked at each other smiling and flew out the door, their first trip to explore their new surroundings."And take the dog with you, she needs some exercise!" she uttered as she opened the door letting Jazzy barrel after them.

The boys walked toward the very back of the lot where there are some trees making up a small woods, perfect for a fort and to defend from their imaginary foes trying to penetrate the outer defenses.

Jazzy walked alongside them until she caught the scent of something she'd never smelled before. She broke off from them and headed to the edge of the yard but they were too focused on which tree would make the best spot for their new fort they didn't notice. Jazzy comes upon a hole in the ground with a wide apron of sand around it, and cautiously peers into the burrow. She sees a set of eyes looking back at her in the darkness, but can't quite make out what it is, sniffing still she is unsure of what this creature is. Being a basset hound, her nose gets her into more mischief than good, and realizing she doesn't have any back up lets out a bark for the boys.

"What did you find Jazzy!", Ciaran calls to her and they both run over to look at the burrow.

"It's a big hole, but I see something in it I think. Let's get mom and dad", Rhys states looking back towards the house. They both excitedly run to the back porch hoping their parents may have an answer to what their new found discovery may be.

Jazzy lingers by the burrow while the boys go inside, when suddenly she hears movement and the eyes in the dark burrow are getting closer. She backs up, unsure what do to when suddenly out comes a tortoise suspiciously looking at her from the mouth of the burrow.

"What are you doing at my burrow?" Jazzy hears as she backs up further.

"I didn't mean to disturb you, I just have never smelled..what.....whatever you are." She stuttered nervously.

" My name is Toast, I'm a gopher tortoise, this is my home." Toast said proudly as she looked around at her burrow. "I've lived in this yard all my life, most of my friends and family lived here too, but they had to move when they built your house...so now I live alone." She said sadly. "Well not all alone, Boris lives over there, but I wouldn't go over there if I was you."

"What's Boris?" Jazzy puzzled as she looked towards the bushes where toast nodded.

"He's mostly all talk, but is usually cranky and in a bad mood." Toast explained. Just then the door opens and Rhys and Ciaran lead their parents out in the yard where Jazzy and Toast are.

" Well would you look at that!, Kids that's a gopher tortoise. They are really special here in Florida because they are known as a keystone species here. They are really important to the ecosystem and provide homes for other animals that share their burrow with them." Dad explained.

"So they run a hotel? " Ciaran asked

"Well yes kind of son, they have a lot of animals come and visit them in their burrows. We need to make sure we give her space and leave her alone. She's going to be a great neighbor for us." He stated as he pulled a tennis ball out of his pocket to lure jazzy away from the burrow.

"This means you too Jazz!" As he throws the ball towards the bushes away from Toast's burrow.

Jazzy quickly changes gears from her introductions with Toast into ball retrieval mode and goes head first into the bushes hoping to get her prized ball back. As she sniffs the ground putting her excellent nose to work in the search, the bushes next to her move.

"Have at you, you foul beast!" she hears and panic sets in and she looks for an escape. She can feel the flapping of wings on her back and then a beak chomps into her tail. She yelps as she gets back into the grass running for her life as her floppy ears wave in the wind.

"Boris!" Toast cries "Be nice to her, she's our new friend!"

Boris stops the attack as he sees the family stand in the yard, Jazzy still running for the back door at full speed. The family sees Boris chasing Jazzy and laughs as they take a few steps back to give Boris and Toast some space.

"Kids that is a burrowing owl, they live in the ground too." Mom states "We need to give them some space, this is a lot of excitement that they aren't used to since no one has lived in this place in awhile. Let's leave them be and get ready for dinner."

"Well we know Jazzy won't have any trouble keeping her distance after that." Dad jokes as they laugh walking back into the house.

"Toast you can't trust these intruders!" Borris exclaimed as he fluffed up.

"They are nice Boris, please behave, you heard them they don't want to bother us, just share the yard with us." Toast remarked scoldingly.

Awakened by the commotion below in the yard Hootenanny peers out of her tree hole to see what's going on. She sees Toast and Boris talking below and the family walking into the house. She flys down to the pair to see what's going on.

"It would be nice to get some sleep around here Boris. Most Owls sleep during the day or have you forgotten that as well as your manners?" Hootenanny scolds and she swoops down.

"I am defending the yard from those foreign invaders. That's not something a lowly screech owl would understand!" Boris proudly states as he puffs up his chest strutting around Toast's burrow. Toast and Hootenanny both roll their eyes as they look away.

"You are ridiculous, Borris." Toast laughed.

The winds start to pick up and a faint crack of thunder can be heard in the distance. Hootenanny looks up at the sky. "It feels like we're going to get a bad storm tonight guys." she surmises as the other two nood in agreement. "We all better head in ''.

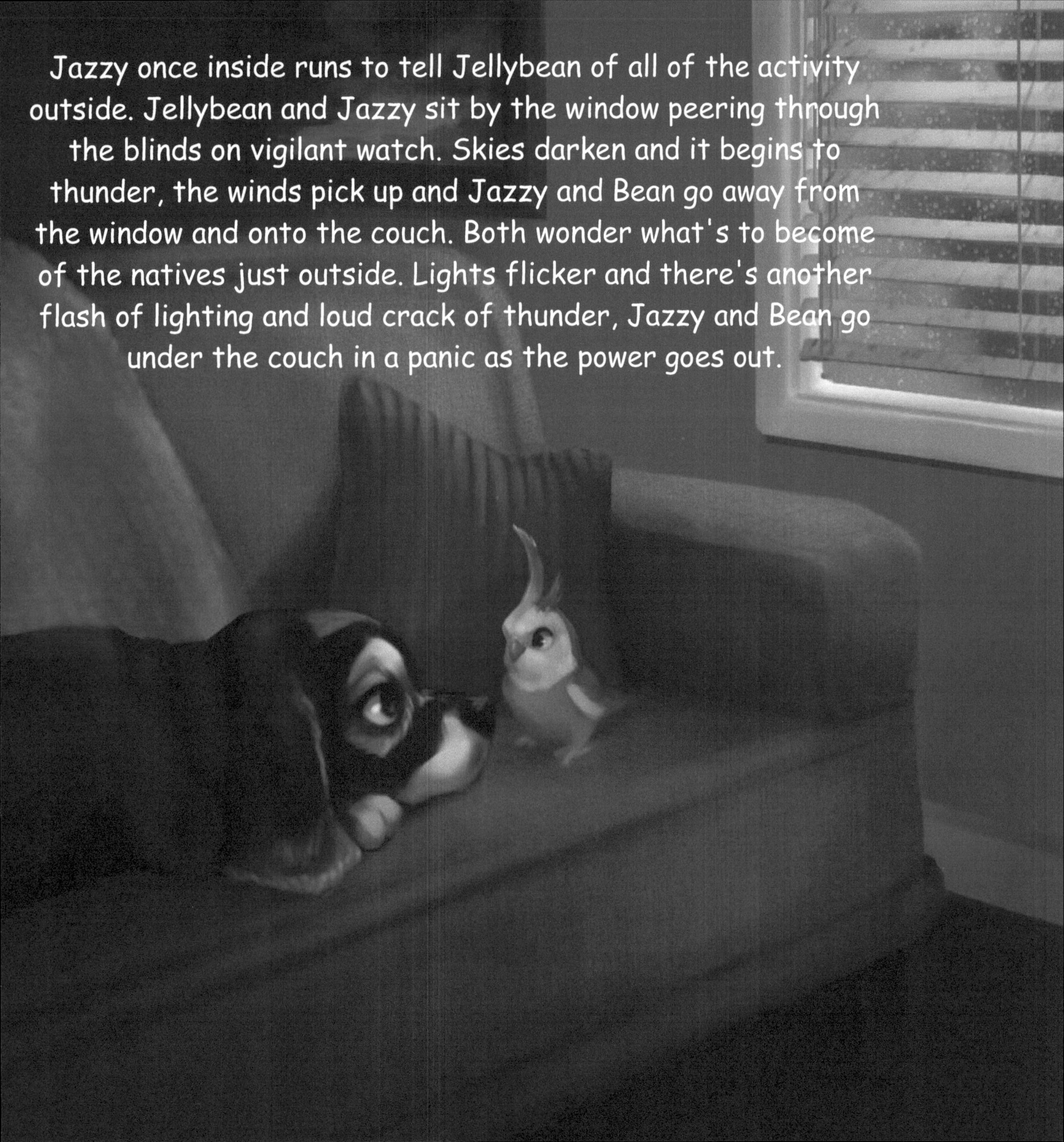

Jazzy once inside runs to tell Jellybean of all of the activity outside. Jellybean and Jazzy sit by the window peering through the blinds on vigilant watch. Skies darken and it begins to thunder, the winds pick up and Jazzy and Bean go away from the window and onto the couch. Both wonder what's to become of the natives just outside. Lights flicker and there's another flash of lighting and loud crack of thunder, Jazzy and Bean go under the couch in a panic as the power goes out.

Next morning the sun rises and a large tree has fallen in the backyard knocking the power lines down. Work crews are going through and clearing debris to restore power to the lines. Hootenanny's house was in the large tree being cut up and Toast's burrow was crushed by the work crews activity. Toast sits in the yard and Hootenanny on the pool fence watching their homes be destroyed.

Jazzy is let out after the work crew leaves the yard and quickly encounters the two looking mournfully at their former homes.

"Hootenanny, this is Jazzy, she's the one Boris chased last night." Toast lamented. "Sorry about Boris Jazzy, he can be a pest."

"I am no such thing!" Boris shreaked through the bushes content to stay in his burrow this time.

Toast and Hootenanny roll their eyes and look back at the storm damage. Jazzy sees the destruction, and starts to think of ways to help her new friends. Suddenly she gets an idea..

"Maybe my family can help." She says, still unsure how exactly. Toast and Hootenanny look at her unconvincingly, as she makes her way back to the house.

Jazzy gets to the back door and barks to be let in, Rhys opens the door but Jazzy runs into the yard as if she wants him to chase her. Both boys stumble into the yard chasing after her, where she leads them to where toast's burrow and Hootenanny's house used to be. The kids quickly go to their parents to show them and it's discovered that their homes have been destroyed by the storm and the work crew's clearing. The family goes inside and starts to look up info on Toast and Hootenanny on the FWC website while Jellybean and Jazzy sit by them, Jellybean perched on a table chewing the mouse cord.

Toast and Hootenanny go to visit Boris, while they try and think of where they should stay and how they should rebuild their homes.

"I just don't have the room ladies, my burrow is not as large as your's was Toast. I don't think we could all fit in there." Boris said disappointed that he couldn't help.

Evening sets in with Hootenanny perched in a tree and toast at the base of it under a palmetto frond as they go to sleep hoping tomorrow will be a better day.

The next morning starts with a racket as both are startled awake with the sound of hammers and screws. Ciaran and Rhys along with their dad are making an owl box for Hootenanny, they paint it and put metal around the tree they see her perched on. The dad gets a ladder and slowly climbs the tree trying not to startle her. She fluffs up and beak clacks in defense. He hangs the box and puts shavings in it, then slowly climbs back down. As he comes down the Ciaran discovers Toast under the palmetto huddled and scared.

"Dad look, the tortoise is under the palmetto by your ladder." Ciaran excitedly says as he points towards Toast hiding in the frawns.

The kids go and find a spot where the Dad digs the starter burrow now far from the tree, toast walks next where they are digging and starts digging her own burrow. The family gives Toast and Hootenanny some space while they play in the pool with Jazzy as Bean watches through the blinds.

"Toast, I don't understand why you don't let them do all the work for you, you literally are digging your own burrow a foot from where they were going to dig one for you?" Borris points out disapprovingly as he watches her work.

"Toast, you literally are digging your own burrow a foot from where they were going to dig one for you?" Borris points out disapprovingly as he watches her work.

"Location, Location, Location, Boris... plus people don't know how to dig right. That is amateur hour work, I'll show you how this is done." Toast says determined as she flings sand onto her new fluffy supervisor.

Later that day, Toast and Hootenanny see Jazzy back out in the yard and excitedly tell her how happy they are with their new homes.....

"Have at you, you floppy eared fiend!" Boris snarls as he pounces from his burrow and flaps as a terrified Jazzy in full retreat.

"Boris behave, she's our friend and you need to be nice to her!" Hootenanny scolds as she fluffs up and scowls at him. Boris grumbles and peers half hidden in his burrow, all that can be seen is the top of his head and his bright golden eyes. Jazzy, thankful for Hootenanny's intervention, trots back into the house for the night to happily tell Jellybean their friends like their new homes.

Like most things in life, routine and a normalcy set in letting time pass. The summer fades to fall and the humidity and rain become less and less. Winter is more of a thought than a season in Florida, so before you know it spring is here and new life can be seen all around.

Our story picks back up with Jazzy going on one of her regular visits to see her friends. As she heads to Toast's burrow she's greeted excitedly by her with great news.

"Jazzy, Hootenanny has a nest!" Toast beams. They both go to the tree and look up at the box as Hootenanny peers down at them

Toast and Jazzy both look up to see four fuzzy owlets peering down at them with Hootenanny beaming proudly.

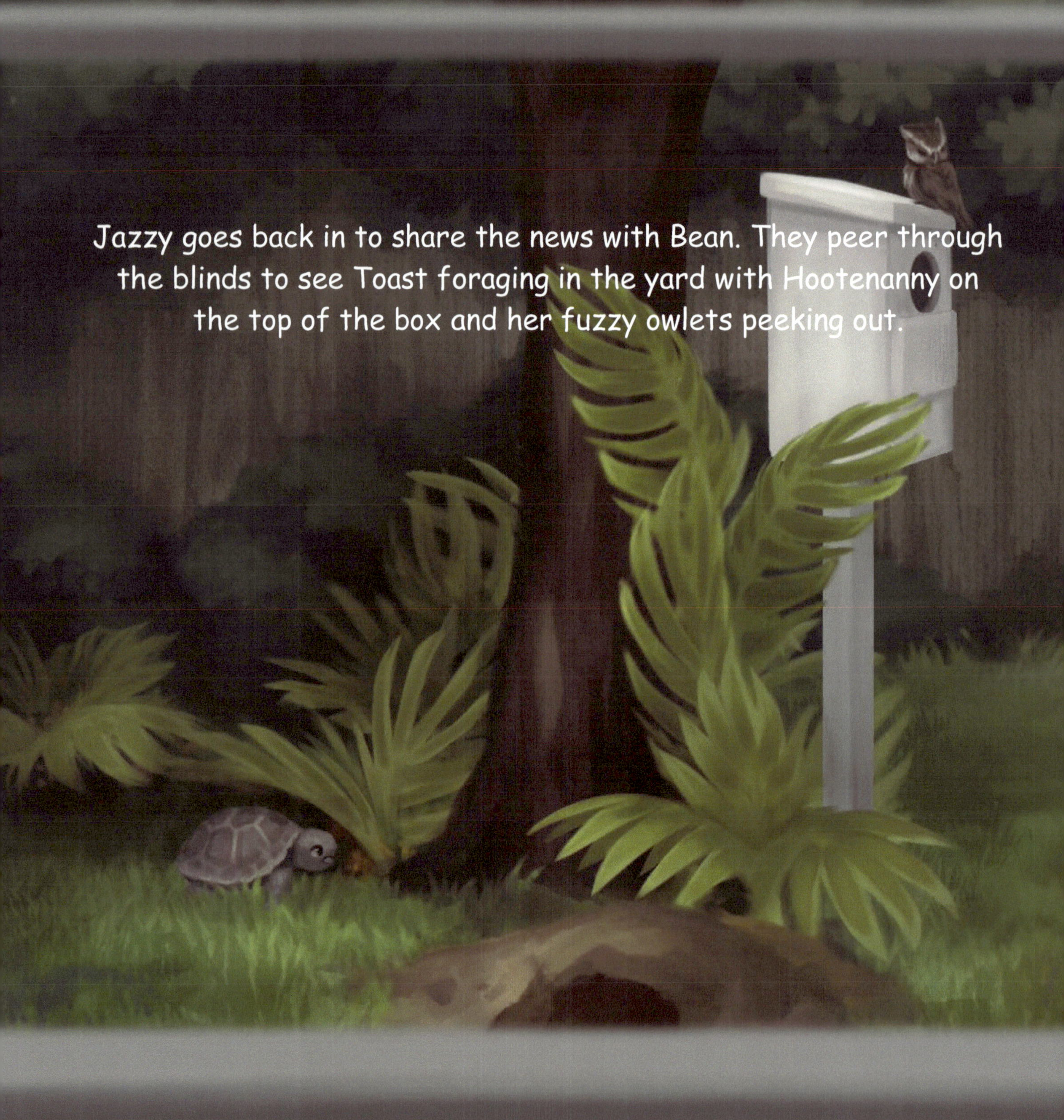

Jazzy goes back in to share the news with Bean. They peer through the blinds to see Toast foraging in the yard with Hootenanny on the top of the box and her fuzzy owlets peeking out.

"Jazzy, friends come in all shapes and sizes, and from the looks of it we're doing pretty well, except for Boris but I think he'll come around." Bean proclaims as they watch the sunset, and listen to the laughter of their family making dinner behind them. Life is good, and these two are just getting into their new adventures........The End.

www.ingramcontent.com/pod-product-compliance
Lightning Source LLC
Chambersburg PA
CBHW042010110726
48006CB00004B/1036
9798836411275